THE WORLD OF
PETER RABBIT™
& FRIENDS
COMPLETE STORY COLLECTION

THE WORLD OF
PETER RABBIT™
& FRIENDS
COMPLETE STORY COLLECTION

From the authorized animated series
based on the original tales

BY BEATRIX POTTER

F. WARNE & CO

FREDERICK WARNE

Published by the Penguin Group
Penguin Books Ltd, 80 Strand, London WC2R 0RL, England
Penguin Putnam Inc., 375 Hudson Street, New York, New York 10014, USA
Penguin Books Australia Ltd, 250 Camberwell Road,
Camberwell, Victoria 3124, Australia
Penguin Books Canada Ltd, 10 Alcorn Avenue, Toronto, Ontario, Canada M4V 3B2
Penguin Books India (P) Ltd, 11 Community Centre,
Panchsheel Park, New Delhi 110 017, India
Penguin Books (NZ) Ltd, Cnr Rosedale and Airborne Roads,
Albany, Auckland, New Zealand
Penguin Books (South Africa) (Pty) Ltd, P O Box 9, Parklands 2121, South Africa
Penguin Books Ltd, Registered Offices: 80 Strand, London WC2R 0RL, England
Web site at: www.peterrabbit.com

This edition first published by Frederick Warne 1999
3 5 7 9 10 8 6 4
This edition copyright © Frederick Warne & Co., 1999
Text copyright © Frederick Warne & Co., 1994, 1996, 1997, 1999
Illustrations from *The World of Peter Rabbit and Friends*™ animated series
copyright © Frederick Warne & Co., 1992, 1993, 1994, 1995, 1996
Frederick Warne & Co. is the owner of all rights, copyrights and trademarks in the
Beatrix Potter character names and illustrations.

ISBN 0 7232 4582 7

Printed and bound in China by Imago Publishing Ltd

CONTENTS

The Tale of Peter Rabbit and Benjamin Bunny   7

The Tale of Tom Kitten and Jemima Puddle-Duck   37

The Tale of Samuel Whiskers   67

The Tailor of Gloucester   97

The Tale of The Flopsy Bunnies and Mrs Tittlemouse   127

The Tale of Mrs Tiggy-Winkle and Mr Jeremy Fisher   151

The Tale of Mr Tod   179

The Tale of Two Bad Mice and Johnny Town-Mouse   203

The Tale of Pigling Bland   235

About *The World of Peter Rabbit & Friends*   265

THE TALE OF
PETER RABBIT
AND
BENJAMIN BUNNY

Once upon a time there were four little rabbits, and their names were Flopsy, Mopsy, Cotton-tail and Peter.

They lived with their mother in a sandbank, underneath the root of a very big fir-tree.

"Now, then," said Mrs Rabbit one morning to her children, "you may go into the fields, or down the lane but don't go into Mr McGregor's garden. Your father had an accident there - he was put in a pie by Mrs McGregor."

"Run along now and don't get into mischief. I'm going out," said Mrs Rabbit.

Then she took her basket and umbrella and went through the wood to the baker.

Flopsy, Mopsy and Cotton-tail, who were good little bunnies, went down the lane to gather blackberries.

But Peter, who was very naughty, ran off towards Mr McGregor's garden. On the way he saw his cousin Benjamin.

"Meet me tomorrow – at the big fir-tree!" Benjamin whispered.

Peter squeezed under the gate into Mr McGregor's garden.

First he ate some lettuces and some French beans; and then he ate some radishes.

"Ooh! My favourite," he said happily.

And then, feeling rather sick, Peter went to look for some parsley.

But whom do you think he should meet round the end of a cucumber frame?

"Oh help!" gasped Peter. "It's Mr McGregor!"

Mr McGregor jumped up and was after Peter in no time, shouting, "Stop, thief!"

Peter was most dreadfully frightened; he rushed all over the garden, for he had forgotten the way back to the gate. He lost his shoes and ran faster on all fours. Indeed, Peter might have got away altogether if he had not run into a gooseberry net.

"Hurry, Peter, hurry," urged some friendly sparrows.

"It's no use," sobbed Peter trying to struggle free, "my brass buttons are all caught up."

Peter rushed into the
toolshed, and jumped
into a watering can.
It would have been
a beautiful thing to
hide in if it had not
had so much water
in it.

"Come on oot, ye wee beastie," muttered Mr McGregor, searching for Peter under the flowerpots.

Suddenly, Peter sneezed, "Kertyschoo!" and Mr McGregor was after him in no time.

Peter jumped out of a window and ran off.

Peter found a door in a wall; but it was locked and there was no room for him to squeeze underneath.

He asked an old mouse the way to the gate, but she had such a large pea in her mouth that she could not answer. Peter began to cry.

Peter came to a pond
where a white cat was
staring at some goldfish.
He crept away quietly; he
had heard about cats from
his cousin, Benjamin Bunny.
  And then Peter saw
the gate!

He ran as fast as he could
and was safe at last in the
wood outside the garden.
  Mr McGregor hung up
the little jacket and shoes
for a scarecrow.

Peter was not very well
during the evening, so his
mother put him to bed and
made some camomile tea.

But Flopsy, Mopsy and
Cotton-tail had bread
and milk and blackberries
for supper.

The next day Benjamin Bunny was sitting on a bank waiting for Peter. Suddenly he heard the trit trot, trit trot of a pony.

"It's Mr and Mrs McGregor going out! I'd better find Peter right away," he thought, and rushed off to find his cousin.

Peter was sitting alone, wrapped only in a red cotton pocket-handkerchief and looking very sorry for himself.

"Who has got your clothes?" said Benjamin.

"The scarecrow in Mr McGregor's garden," replied Peter and he told Benjamin what had happened the day before.

Little Benjamin laughed. "That's what I came to tell you. Mr McGregor has gone out, *and* Mrs McGregor."

23

They made their way to
Mr McGregor's garden
and got up onto the wall.
Peter's coat and shoes
were plainly to be seen on
the scarecrow, topped with
an old tam-o-shanter of
Mr McGregor's.

"It spoils people's clothes
to squeeze under a gate," said
Benjamin. "The proper way
to get in, is to climb down a
pear tree."

Little Benjamin said that
the first thing to be done was
to get back Peter's clothes.

Then he suggested that they should fill the handkerchief with onions as a present for his Aunt. Peter was not enjoying himself.

But Benjamin was quite at home and ate a lettuce leaf. Peter said he should like to go. Then he dropped half the onions!

But as they turned a corner, Peter and Benjamin
stopped suddenly.

"Gracious, what now, Benjamin?" asked Peter.

This is what those little rabbits saw round the corner!

"Quick, under here," whispered Benjamin. "She's coming towards us."

Perhaps the cat liked the smell of onions – because she sat down on top of the basket.

She sat there for *five hours*!

Mrs Rabbit was getting anxious.

"Mr Bouncer, have you seen my son, Peter? He's been missing all day."

"Benjamin has taken himself off too," replied Benjamin's father. "Leave it to me, ma'am, I think I know where the young rascals have got to. And if I'm right . . ."

"Father!" shouted Benjamin from beneath the basket.

The cat looked up and saw Mr Bouncer prancing along the top of the wall. Mr Bouncer had no opinion whatever of cats. He kicked her into the greenhouse and locked the door.

31

Mr Bouncer pulled Benjamin from beneath the basket.

"Benjamin first, I think, then Peter . . . Off home with you now."

Then Mr Bouncer took the handkerchief of onions, and marched those two naughty rabbits all the way home.

"Well, at least you've found your jacket and shoes, Peter," said Mrs Rabbit, relieved to see her son home safely.

"There now my dears," she added, "all's well that ends well. But let that be a lesson to you, Peter."

THE TALE OF
TOM KITTEN
AND
JEMIMA
PUDDLE~DUCK

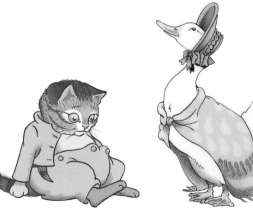

Once upon a time there were three little kittens, and their names were Mittens, Tom Kitten and Moppet.

They had dear little coats of their own; and they tumbled about the doorstep and played in the dust.

"I do wish Mrs Twitchit would keep her kittens in order," quacked Jemima Puddle-duck.

One day their mother – Mrs Tabitha Twitchit – expected friends to tea; so she fetched her kittens indoors, to wash and dress them before her visitors arrived.

First she scrubbed their faces and then she brushed their fur.

She dressed Mittens and Moppet in clean pinafores.

Then it was Tom's turn.
"Goodness me, I had not realised quite how much you have grown!" sighed Mrs Tabitha Twitchit as several buttons burst off. She sewed the buttons back on again, and Tom was squeezed into his best suit.

41

"Now keep your frocks clean, children," said Mrs Tabitha Twitchit. "You must walk on your hind legs. Keep away from the dirty ash-pit. And from the pigstye - oh, *and* the Puddle-ducks," she continued.

Then she let the kittens out into the garden to be out of the way.

"Let's climb up the rockery, and sit on the garden wall," suggested Moppet eagerly.

Moppet's white tucker fell down into the road. "Never mind," she said, "we can fetch it later. Now, where's Tom?"

"He's still down there," said Mittens, pointing to the rockery below them.

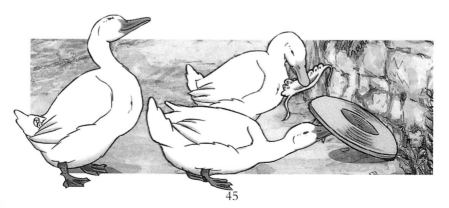

Tom was in pieces when he reached the top of the
wall. His hat fell off and the rest of his buttons burst.

While Mittens and Moppet tried to pull him together
there was a pit pat paddle-pat! and three Puddle-ducks
came along the road. They caught sight of the kittens'
clothes lying at the bottom of the wall!

"Rather fetching, don't you agree, Jemima?" asked Rebeccah, as she tried on Tom's hat.

Mittens laughed so much that she fell off the wall. Moppet and Tom followed her down.

"Come and help me to dress Tom," said Moppet to Mr Drake Puddle-duck.

But Mr Drake put Tom's clothes on *himself*.

"It is a very fine morning," he said and he and Jemima and Rebeccah Puddle-duck set off up the road, keeping step - pit pat, paddle pat!

Then Mrs Tabitha Twitchit came down the garden path
and saw her kittens on the wall with no clothes on.

"Oh, my goodness," she gasped, "just look at you!
My friends will arrive any moment and you are not fit
to be seen – I am affronted!

"Straight to your room and not one sound do I wish
to hear," she ordered.

When Mrs Tabitha Twitchit's friends arrived I am sorry to say she told them that her kittens were in bed with the measles; which was not true.

"Dear, dear. What a shame. The poor souls," exclaimed Henrietta.

But the kittens were not in bed; *not* in the least.

At the tea-party, strange noises were heard from above. "You did say they were poorly, didn't you, Tabitha dear?" asked Cousin Ribby curiously.

As for the Puddle-ducks,
they went into a pond.
The clothes all came off
because there were no
buttons, and they have
been looking for them
ever since.

Indeed, Jemima was no better
at finding things than she was
at hiding them. She had often
tried to hide her eggs, but
they were always found and
carried off. No-one believed
that Jemima had the patience
to sit on her eggs.

Poor Jemima became
quite desperate.

"I *will* hatch my own eggs, if I have to make a nest right away from the farm," she said.

So, one fine spring afternoon, Jemima put on her best bonnet and shawl and set off."

Jemima waddled about in search of a nesting place. Suddenly she was startled to find an elegantly dressed gentleman reading a newspaper.

"I am trying to find a convenient, dry nesting place so that I may sit on my eggs," said Jemima.

"Indeed! How interesting! As to a nest there is no difficulty: I have a sackful of feathers in my wood-shed," said the bushy long-tailed gentleman. He opened the door to show Jemima.

"You will be in nobody's way. You may sit there as long as you like," he assured her.

"Goodness," thought Jemima. "I've never seen so many feathers in one place. Very comfortable, though, and perfect for making my nest, so warm . . . so dry."

The sandy-whiskered gentleman promised to take great care of Jemima's nest until she came back again the next day.

Jemima Puddle-duck came every afternoon, and laid nine eggs in the nest. The foxy gentleman admired them immensely.

At last Jemima told the gentleman she was ready to sit
on her eggs until they hatched.

"Madam," he said, "before you commence your tedious
sitting I intend to give you a treat. Let us have a dinner
party all to ourselves. May I ask you to bring some herbs
from the farm garden to make, er . . . a savoury omelette?
I will provide lard for the stuff . . . I mean, omelette."

Jemima Puddle-duck was a simpleton; she quite unsuspectingly went round nibbling snippets off all the different sorts of herbs that are used for stuffing roast duck.

"What are you doing with those onions?" asked Kep, the collie dog. "And where do you go every afternoon by yourself?"

Jemima told him the whole story.

"Now, exactly where is your nest?" enquired Kep suspiciously.

Jemima went up the cart-road for the last time and flew over the wood.

"Come into the house as soon as you've looked at your eggs," ordered the bushy long-tailed gentleman rather sharply. Jemima had never heard him speak like that. She felt surprised and uncomfortable.

While Jemima was inside
she heard pattering feet
round the back of the shed.
She became much alarmed.
"Oh, what shall I do?"
she worried.

A moment afterwards there were the most awful noises – barking, baying, growls and howls, squealing and groans.

"And I think that is the last we will see of that foxy-whiskered gentleman," said Kep.

Unfortunately the puppies had gobbled up all of Jemima's eggs before Kep could stop them.

Poor Jemima Puddle-duck was escorted home in tears on account of those eggs.

Jemima laid some more eggs in June and she was allowed to keep them herself; but only four of them hatched. She said that it was because of her nerves, but she had always been a bad sitter.

THE TALE OF
SAMUEL
WHISKERS

Once upon a time there was an old cat, called
Mrs Tabitha Twitchit, who was an anxious parent.
She used to lose her kittens continually, and whenever
they were lost they were always in mischief!

On baking day Mrs Tabitha Twitchit determined to shut her kittens in a cupboard. She caught Moppet and Mittens . . .

but she could not find Tom.

Tom Kitten looked around for a convenient place to hide and fixed upon the chimney.

Inside the chimney, Tom coughed and choked with the smoke. He began to climb right to the top.

While Mrs Tabitha Twitchit was searching for Tom, Moppet and Mittens pushed open the cupboard door. They went straight to the dough which was set to rise in a pan in front of the fire. "Shall we make dear little muffins?" said Mittens to Moppet.

But just at that moment, somebody knocked at the door.

"Oh, come in Cousin Ribby. I'm in sad trouble. I've lost my dear son Thomas. I'm afraid the rats have got him," sobbed Mrs Tabitha Twitchit. "And now Moppet and Mittens are gone too. What it is to have an unruly family," she wailed.

"Well Cousin, we shan't find any of them standing here," said Ribby firmly. "I'm not afraid of rats. I'll help you find Tom - and whip him too. Now, just where would a naughty kitten hide?"

Meanwhile, up the chimney Tom Kitten was getting very frightened! It was quite confusing in the dark, and he felt quite lost.

All at once he fell head
over heels down a hole
and landed on a heap of
very dirty rags.

Opposite to him – as far
away as he could sit – was
an enormous rat.

"How dare you tumble into my bed all covered with smuts!" said the rat (whose name was Samuel Whiskers).

"Please sir, the chimney wants sweeping," said poor Tom Kitten.

"Anna Maria! Anna Maria!" Samuel Whiskers called.
There was a pattering noise and an old woman rat
poked her head round a rafter.

"What have we here, Samuel?" she asked. "A tasty morsel indeed!" She rushed upon Tom and before he knew what was happening, he was rolled up in a bundle, and tied with string in very tight knots.

"Anna Maria," said the old man rat, "make me a kitten dumpling roly-poly pudding for my dinner."

"Hmm . . . it requires dough and a pat of butter and a rolling-pin," said Anna Maria.

The two rats consulted together for a few minutes and then went away.

Samuel Whiskers went boldly down the front staircase to the dairy to get the butter.

He made a second journey for the rolling-pin.

82

Anna Maria went to the kitchen to steal the dough. She borrowed a small saucer, and scooped up the dough with her paws.

The rats set to work. They smeared Tom Kitten with butter, and then they rolled him in the dough.

Meanwhile, Ribby found Moppet hiding in a flour barrel.

"Mother," cried Moppet, "there's been an old woman rat in the kitchen and she's stolen some of the dough!"

Mittens was found in the dairy, hiding in an empty jar.

"There's been an old man rat in the dairy, mother. He's stolen a pat of butter and a rolling-pin!" Mittens cried.

"Oh my poor son, Thomas!" exclaimed Tabitha, wringing her paws.

Ribby and Mrs Tabitha Twitchit rushed upstairs.
They could hear a roly-poly noise quite distinctly
under the attic floor. "We must send for John Joiner
at once, with a saw!" said Ribby.

All this time, the two rats had been hard at work.

"Will not the string be very indigestible, Anna Maria?" inquired Samuel Whiskers.

"No, no. It is of no consequence," she replied. "But I do wish he would hold his head still."

"Oh, Mr Joiner, this way,"
said Cousin Ribby. "We can
hear the strangest sounds . . .
I dread to think! Come along,
follow me quickly now."

"I do not think it will be a good pudding," said Samuel Whiskers, looking at Tom Kitten. "It smells sooty."

Anna Maria was about to argue the point, when they heard noises up above – the rasping of a saw, and the noise of a little dog, scratching and yelping!

"We are discovered and interrupted, Anna Maria. Let us collect our property (and other people's) and depart at once. I fear that we shall be obliged to leave this pudding, but I am persuaded that the knots would have proved indigestible," said Samuel Whiskers.

91

So it happened that by the time John Joiner had got the plank up there was nobody under the floor except the rolling-pin and Tom Kitten in a very dirty dumpling!

Samuel Whiskers and Anna Maria found a wheelbarrow belonging to Miss Potter which they borrowed and hastily filled with a quantity of bundles.

Then Samuel Whiskers and Anna Maria made their way to Farmer Potatoes' hay barn and hauled their parcels with a bit of string to the top of the hay mow.

The cat family quickly recovered. The dumpling was peeled off Tom Kitten and made separately into a pudding, with currants in it to hide the smuts. They had to put Tom Kitten into a hot bath to get the butter off.

And after that, there were no more rats for a long time at Mrs Tabitha Twitchit's.

THE
TAILOR
OF
GLOUCESTER

Once upon a time there was an old tailor who lived in Gloucester.

He sat in the window of a little shop in Westgate Street, cross-legged on a table, from morning till night.

One bitter cold day near Christmas, the tailor began to make a coat of cherry-coloured corded silk.

"The finest of wedding-coats for the Mayor of Gloucester who is to be married on Christmas Day in the morning," he muttered to himself as he worked.

The table was all littered with cherry-coloured snippets.

"I'm sure I cannot afford to waste the smallest piece," said the tailor as he continued cutting. "Too narrow breadths for nought except waistcoats for mice!

"Now the lining . . . Ah yes! Just the thing – yellow taffeta."

Unnoticed, little mice retrieved the scraps from his work bench and carried them off.

"By my whiskers, I cannot remember when we had silk of such quality on these premises!" exclaimed the little mouse.

"Oh, yellow taffeta – just what I would have chosen myself," whispered another.

"My poor back," sighed the tailor, "but it is done. The light is fading and I am tired. All is ready to sew in the morning, except for one little item - I am wanting one single skein of cherry-coloured twisted silk thread."

The old tailor locked up his shop and shuffled home through the snow.

The mice were more fortunate and did not have to brave the cold. Using secret passages and staircases behind the wooden wainscots of all the old houses in Gloucester, they could run from house to house.

The tailor lived alone with his cat, whose name was
Simpkin. All day long, while the tailor was out at work,
Simpkin kept house by himself. Simpkin was also fond
of the mice, but he gave them no satin for coats!

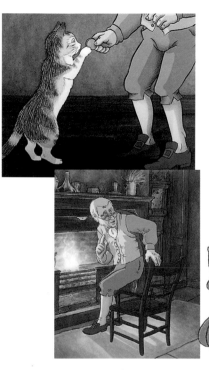

"Ah, Simpkin, old friend!" exclaimed the tailor as he arrived home. "We shall make our fortune from this coat, but I am worn to a ravelling. Take this groat (which is our last fourpence) and buy a penn'orth of bread, a penn'orth of milk and a penn'orth of sausages."

"And with the last penny buy me one penn'orth of cherry-coloured silk. But do not lose the last penny, Simpkin, for I have *no more twist*."

Weary from his day's work, the tailor sat by the fire and began to dream about that beautiful coat.

Suddenly, his thoughts were interrupted by a number of little noises coming from the dresser at the other side of the kitchen – *Tip tap, tip tap tip!*

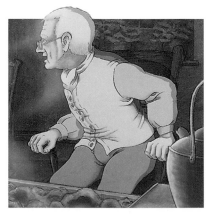

Tip tap, tip tap tip!
   "Now what can that be?" the tailor wondered.
He crossed the kitchen, and stood quite still beside the
dresser, listening and peering through his spectacles.

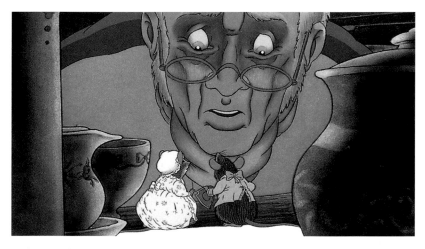

The tailor lifted up a teacup which was upside-down.
Out stepped a little live lady mouse. Then, out from
under the teacups, bowls and basins, stepped more and
more little mice. "This is very peculiar," remarked the
tailor. "I'll wager this is all
Simpkin's doing, the rascal.

"Oh, was I wise to
entrust my last fourpence
to him? And was it right to
let loose those mice? Alack!
I am undone!"

Simpkin opened the door with an angry "G-r-r-miaw!"
for he hated the snow.

He sniffed and then
looked suspiciously at the
dresser – the cups and jugs
had been moved! Simpkin
wanted his supper of a
little fat mouse.

"Simpkin," asked the tailor
anxiously, "where is my twist?"
Simpkin was cross with his master. He quickly hid
the twist in the teapot on the dresser, and growled
at the tailor.

"Where is my twist, Simpkin? Alack, I am undone . . .
I am weak," lamented the tailor and went sadly to bed.

The poor old tailor was very
ill with fever. Tossing and turning
in bed he mumbled -
"No more twist . . . one-and-twenty
buttonholes . . . to be finished by
noon on Saturday . . . and it is
already Tuesday!"

Indeed, what should become of the cherry-coloured coat?

In the tailor's shop the embroidered silk and satin lay cut out upon the table, and who should come to sew them when the window was barred and the door was fast locked?

The tailor lay ill for three days and three nights
and then it was Christmas Eve and very late at night.
The moon climbed up over the roofs and chimneys.
All the city of Gloucester was fast asleep under the snow.

The cathedral clock struck twelve and Simpkin went
out into the night.

For an old story tells how all the animals can talk in the night between Christmas Eve and Christmas Day in the morning (though very few people can hear them, or know what it is they say).

Simpkin wandered through the streets feeling lonely and hungry.

But when Simpkin turned a corner he saw a glow of light coming from the tailor's shop. He crept up to peep in at the window.

Inside the shop was a snippeting of scissors and a snappeting of thread and little mouse voices were singing loudly and happily: "Three little mice sat down to spin, Pussy passed by and she peeped in."

Simpkin miawed to get in but the door was locked.

"Dear me, and the key is under the tailor's pillow," mocked a little mouse seamstress gleefully.

Simpkin came away from the shop and went home. There he found the poor old tailor without fever, sleeping peacefully.

Simpkin went on tip-toe and took a little parcel of silk out of the teapot - he felt quite ashamed of his badness compared with those good little mice!

When the tailor awoke the next morning, he saw the skein of cherry-coloured twisted silk, and beside it the repentant Simpkin!

The tailor went to his shop.

"Alack, I have my twist, but no more strength, nor time, for this is Christmas Day in the morning! The Mayor of Gloucester is to be married by noon – and where is his cherry-coloured coat?"

He unlocked the door of the little shop and looked in amazement.

There, where he had left plain cuttings of silk lay the most beautiful coat and embroidered satin waistcoat.

Everything was finished except for one single cherry-coloured buttonhole, where there was pinned a scrap of paper with these words - in little teeny weeny writing - NO MORE TWIST.

And from then began the luck of the Tailor of Gloucester. He grew quite stout, and he grew quite rich.

Never were seen such ruffles, or such embroidered cuffs. But his buttonholes were the greatest triumph – the stitches were so neat and so small they looked as if they had been made by little mice!

THE TALE OF
THE FLOPSY BUNNIES

AND MRS TITTLEMOUSE

When Benjamin Bunny grew up, he married his
Cousin Flopsy. They had a large family, and they were
very improvident and cheerful. I do not remember the
separate names of their children; they were generally
called the "Flopsy Bunnies".

As there was not always quite enough to eat,
Benjamin used to borrow cabbages from Flopsy's
brother, Peter Rabbit, who kept a nursery garden.

And when Peter Rabbit had no cabbages to spare,
the Flopsy Bunnies went across the field to a rubbish
heap, in the ditch outside Mr McGregor's garden.

Mr McGregor's rubbish heap was a mixture – jam pots, paper bags, rotten marrows and an old boot or two. One day - oh joy! - there were a quantity of overgrown lettuces.

A little wood-mouse was picking over the rubbish. Her name was Thomasina Tittlemouse.

"Please excuse my youngsters," said Benjamin, "they have waited overlong for their lunch today!"

"Then I think I shall go home," said Mrs Tittlemouse, "before I am eaten in mistake for a lettuce!"

Mrs Tittlemouse lived alone in a bank under a hedge. Such a funny house!

There were yards and yards of sandy passages, leading to storerooms and nut and seed cellars.

There was a kitchen, a parlour, a pantry, and a larder. Also, there was Mrs Tittlemouse's bedroom, where she slept in a little box bed!

Mrs Tittlemouse was a most terribly particular little mouse, always sweeping and dusting the soft sandy floors.

One day a little old woman ran up and down in a red spotty cloak. "Your house is on fire, Mother Ladybird! Fly away home!"

Another day, a big fat spider came in to shelter from the rain. "Go away, you bold bad spider! Leaving ends of cobweb all over my nice clean house!"

Mrs Tittlemouse went to a distant storeroom to fetch cherry stones and thistle-down seed.

Suddenly, round a corner, she met Babbitty Bumble and several other bees, buzzing fiercely. "What an intrusion!" said Mrs Tittlemouse crossly. "I will ask Mr Benjamin Bunny to help me drive out these tiresome bees!"

The Flopsy Bunnies simply stuffed lettuces and one after another, they were overcome with slumber. Benjamin was not so much overcome as his children. Before going to sleep he was sufficiently wide awake to put a paper bag over his head to keep off the flies. Mrs Tittlemouse rustled across the paper bag, and awakened Benjamin Bunny.

"Mr Benjamin, I am so sorry to disturb you, but I thought to ask a favour of you."

Benjamin stirred sleepily.

Then they heard a heavy tread above their heads. Mr McGregor was approaching!

"The Flopsy Bunnies! Mr McGregor is sure to see the Flopsy Bunnies," said Mrs Tittlemouse. "We must wake them up, we must warn them!" But it was impossible to wake the Flopsy Bunnies.

A robin darted around
Mr McGregor's head, trying to
distract him. Suddenly, he emptied out
a sackful of lawn mowings right upon
the top of the sleeping Flopsy Bunnies!

Mr McGregor looked down
and saw some funny little
brown tips of ears sticking up
through the lawn mowings.

Presently a fly settled on one of them and it moved. Mr McGregor climbed down onto the rubbish heap – "One, two, three, four! five! six leetle rabbits!" said he as he dropped them into his sack.

Mr McGregor tied up the sack and left it on the wall. He went to put away the mowing machine.

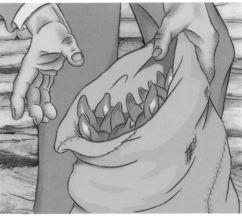

Then Mrs Tittlemouse came out of her jam pot, and
Benjamin took the paper bag off his head. They could
see the sack, up on the wall. Just then Mrs Flopsy Bunny
(who had remained at home) came across the field.

"Mr McGregor has caught your babies and put them in this sack!" said Mrs Tittlemouse.

Benjamin and Flopsy were in despair; they could not undo the string.

But Mrs Tittlemouse was a resourceful person. She nibbled a hole in the bottom corner of the sack!

The little rabbits were pulled out and pinched to wake them.

Their parents stuffed the empty sack with three rotten vegetable marrows, an old blacking-brush and two decayed turnips. Then they all hid under a bush and watched for Mr McGregor.

Mr McGregor came back to fetch the sack, believing that the Flopsy Bunnies were still sleeping inside. But if he had looked behind he would have seen them following at a safe distance!

They watched him go into his house . . .

Mr McGregor threw down the sack on the stone floor. "One, two, three, four, five, six leetle rabbits!" said Mr McGregor.

Mrs McGregor untied the sack and put her hand inside. When she felt the vegetables she became very very angry.

A rotten marrow came flying through the window, and hit the youngest Flopsy Bunny.

Benjamin and Flopsy decided that it was time to go home.

When Mrs Tittlemouse got back to the parlour,
she heard someone coughing in a fat voice, and
there sat Mr Jackson! "Deary me,
you have got very wet feet!"
said Mrs Tittlemouse.

He sat and smiled, and the
water dripped off his coat tails.
Mrs Tittlemouse went round
with a mop.

He sat such a while that he had to be asked if he would take some dinner? First she offered him some cherry stones. "No teeth, no teeth!" mumbled Mr Jackson.

"Thistledown seed?" said Mrs Tittlemouse.

"Tiddly, widdly, widdly! Pouff, pouff, puff!" said Mr Jackson, blowing thistledown all over the room. Then he rose from the table and began to look in the cupboards for some honey. Mrs Tittlemouse followed with a dish-cloth.

They went along the sandy passage. Mr Jackson met Babbitty Bumble round a corner, and snapped her up, and put her down again.

"I do not like bumble bees, they are all over bristles," said Mr Jackson, wiping his mouth with his coat sleeve.

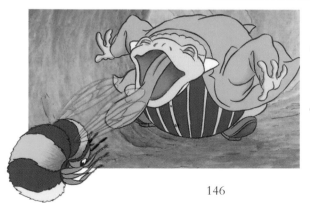

"I shall go distracted!" scolded Mrs Tittlemouse.

Mr Jackson pulled out the bees nest and ate the honey. The bees gathered up their pollen-bags and flew away to find a quieter place for their nest. Mrs Tittlemouse shut herself in the nut cellar.

When she ventured out everybody had gone away. But the untidiness was something dreadful! She went out and fetched some twigs, to partly close up the front door.

But she was too tired to do any more. She fell asleep in her chair.

Next morning she got up very early and did a spring cleaning which lasted a fortnight.

When it was all neat and clean, she gave a party to five other mice. Mr Jackson could not squeeze in at the door. So they handed him out acorn-cupfuls of honey-dew through the window and he was not at all offended.

The Flopsy Bunnies did not forget Mrs Tittlemouse.
Next Christmas Thomasina Tittlemouse got a present of
enough rabbit-wool to make herself a cloak and a hood,
and a handsome muff and a pair of warm mittens.

THE TALE OF
MRS TIGGY~WINKLE
AND
MR JEREMY FISHER

Once upon a time there was a little girl called Lucie,
who lived at a farm called Little-town. She was a good
little girl - only she was *always* losing her handkerchiefs!
"That's three handkins and a pinafore. Oh dear!
Have you seen them, Tabby Kitten?"

The kitten went on washing her white paws; so Lucie asked a speckled hen - "Sally Henny-Penny, have you found three pocket-handkins?"

But the speckled hen ran away, clucking.

Then Lucie asked Cock Robin. He looked sideways at Lucie with his bright black eye, and flew over a stile and away.

Lucie scrambled up the hill as fast as her stout legs would carry her. "Excuse me sir," Lucie asked Mr Jeremy Fisher, "have you seen my pocket-handkins?"

"I'm afraid not, young lady," he replied.

Then Lucie saw some pieces of white on the hillside. "They might just be my pocket-handkins," she said.

Presently Lucie came to a spring, bubbling out from the hillside. "Goodness! Who could have put such a tiny bucket there - it's no bigger than an egg-cup! And look at those little foot-marks," remarked Lucie. She followed the footprints until she came to a little door in the hillside.

Lucie knocked – once – twice, and a little frightened
voice called out "Oh! Who's that?"

"I'm Lucie. I didn't mean to startle you, but who
are you? And have you seen my pocket-handkins?"

"Oh, yes, if you please'm. My name is Mrs Tiggy-winkle. Please do make yourself comfortable," said the little person and she started to iron something.

"What's that?" asked Lucie. "That's not my pocket handkin."

"Oh no," Mrs Tiggy-winkle replied, "that's a little scarlet waistcoat belonging to Cock Robin."

"And if you please'm, that's a damask tablecloth belonging to Jenny Wren."

"There's one of my pocket handkins!" cried Lucie, "and there's my pinny!"

"Fancy that!" said Mrs Tiggy-winkle, "they were there all the time. I'll just put the iron over them."

"There!" exclaimed Mrs Tiggy-winkle proudly, holding up Lucie's newly ironed pinny.

"Oh, that *is* lovely!" said Lucie.

"Goodness, what are they?" asked Lucie pointing to some long yellow things.

"That's a pair of stockings belonging to Sally Henny-penny."

"There's another handkersniff, but it's red," said Lucie.

"That one belongs to Mrs Rabbit and it did so smell of onions, I've had to wash it separately."

"And these are woolly coats belonging to the little lambs at Skelghyl. Now then, I always have to starch these little dicky shirt-fronts. They're Tom Titmouse's and he's most terrible particular."

"I'll just hang these up to air. I'd take it very kindly'm if you would hand the things up to me."

Lucie held up a tattered blue jacket.

"Now there's a story," said Mrs Tiggy-winkle. "Young master Peter Rabbit had a narrow escape from Mr McGregor's garden, but his jacket was left behind, and what with the rain and all . . ."

Then Mrs Tiggy-winkle made some tea – a cup for herself and a cup for Lucie.

Afterwards they tied up all the clothes in bundles and set off to deliver the clean washing.

Very soon there was nothing left to carry except one little bundle that belonged to Mr Jeremy Fisher.

"I do believe I saw him fishing when I was searching for my handkins," said Lucie as they approached the little house by the pond.

"Ladies, ahoy," greeted Mr Jeremy Fisher.

"I was just about to leave your clean washing and collect from the porch as usual," said Mrs Tiggy-winkle.

"Ah yes, little mishap," said Mr Jeremy, as Mrs Tiggy-winkle held up his torn mackintosh. ". . . er, more of an accident . . . very nearly fatal."

"A really frightful thing it would have been - but let me start from the beginning . . . " and Mr Jeremy began to tell his story.

The day had started so well for Mr Jeremy Fisher.

"Ah! Nice drop of rain, be good fishing today I shouldn't wonder. I will get some worms and catch a dish of minnows for my dinner. If I catch more than five fish, I will invite my friends Mr Alderman Ptolemy Tortoise and Sir Isaac Newton."

"Now then, my mackintosh, and goloshes. Mmm . . . where did I leave my sandwiches?"

Mr Jeremy Fisher set off with hops to the place where he kept his boat.

"I know just the place for minnows," he said and pushed the boat into open water.

He settled himself cross-legged and arranged his fishing tackle.

The rain trickled down his back and for nearly an hour
he stared at the float. "This is getting tiresome. I foresee,
I fear, an adjustment to the dinner menu. I will eat a
butterfly sandwich and wait till the shower is over."

But then, a great water-beetle came up underneath the lily leaf and tweaked the toe of one of Mr Jeremy's goloshes.
And all at once he heard a splash from the bank.
"I trust that is not a rat," he said crossly. "Is there no peace to be had anywhere?" and he punted off to find a quieter spot.

A little girl asked him if he'd seen her lost handkins.

"I'm afraid not, young lady," he replied. "Dear me, whatever would I be doing with pocket handkins, indeed," he chuckled.

Just then there was a
bobbing of the float and
a tugging of the line.
"A minnow! A minnow!
I have him by the nose!"

But Mr Jeremy Fisher
got a horrible surprise.
He had landed little Jack
Sharp, the stickleback.

"Ouch! Jack Sharp – what are you doing on the end
of my line? Get off my boat this instant!"

Mr Jeremy sat on the edge of his boat – when suddenly, a *much* worse thing happened.
An enormous trout came up - ker-pflop-p-p-p! - and seized Mr Jeremy with a snap. Then it turned and dived down to the bottom of the pond!

Luckily the trout did not like the taste of Mr Jeremy Fisher's mackintosh and spat him out again. He scrambled out onto the nearest bank.

"Never, never, have I been so glad to see the light of day," he gasped. "What a mercy it was not a pike! Just look at my best mackintosh – all in tatters."

". . . And that is what happened," finished Mr Jeremy Fisher. "It was a nightmare, I assure you, truly frightful."

"Oh, mercy me!" exclaimed Mrs Tiggy-winkle anxiously.

"Oh, Miss Lucie," said Mrs Tiggy-winkle,
"here are Mr Jeremy Fisher's guests.
We must be on our way. I will do
my best with your things sir."

Mr Jeremy and his friends sat
down to dinner. "Perhaps we
might take a glass of pond
wine with our roast grasshopper
and ladybird sauce?"

And Mrs Tiggy-winkle hurried home, not stopping
to give Lucie a bill for the washing.

Lucie watched her as she went and wondered,
"But where is your cap and your shawl and your gown?
If I didn't know better, Mrs Tiggy-winkle, I would think
that you were nothing but a hedgehog!"

THE TALE OF
MR TOD

*A story about two disagreeable people
called Tommy Brock and Mr Tod*

Old Mr Bouncer sat in the spring sunshine smoking a pipe of rabbit tobacco.

He lived with his son Benjamin Bunny and his daughter-in-law Flopsy, who had a young family.

"Now take care of the children Uncle Bouncer," said Flopsy, "we're going out."

The little rabbit-babies were just old enough to open their blue eyes and kick. They lay in a fluffy bed of rabbit wool and hay. To tell the truth – old Mr Bouncer had forgotten them.

He sat in the sun, and conversed with Tommy Brock, who was passing through the wood with a sack and a little spade which he used for digging, and some mole traps. Tommy Brock was friendly with old Mr Bouncer; they agreed in disliking Mr Tod. "My dear old chap, won't you step inside for a slice of seed cake and a glass of homemade cowslip wine?" said Mr Bouncer.

Tommy Brock squeezed himself into
the rabbit hole with alacrity. "Have a
cabbage leaf cigar, Tommy," said old
Mr Bouncer. Smoke filled the burrow.
Old Mr Bouncer coughed and
laughed; Tommy Brock puffed
and grinned.

   Then Mr Bouncer slumped
lower in his chair and shut his
eyes because of the smoke . . .

Tommy Brock
waited a few
moments to be
sure that old
Mr Bouncer
was fast asleep.
Then he put
all the young
rabbit-babies
into his sack.

When Flopsy and
Benjamin came
back, old Mr
Bouncer woke up.
"Where are the
children?" said
Flopsy, anxiously.
Mr Bouncer
would not confess
that he had
admitted anybody
into the burrow.

The smell of badger was undeniable, and there were round heavy footmarks in the sand. Mr Bouncer was in disgrace; Flopsy rung her ears, and slapped him. "It's old Tommy Brock, he's taken our babies," she cried.

"Now don't worry, Flopsy," said Benjamin, "I'll catch that old rogue." Benjamin Bunny set off at once after Tommy Brock.

Benjamin soon found Tommy Brock's footmarks.

The path led to a part of the thicket where the trees had been cleared. Benjamin stopped suddenly – Mr Tod's stick house was before him and, for once,

Mr Tod was at home. Inside the stick house somebody dropped a plate. Benjamin stamped his foot, and bolted.

He never stopped until he came to the other side of the wood. Tommy Brock had turned the same way. Upon the top of the wall, some ravellings of a sack had caught on a bush.

It was getting late in the afternoon.
Other rabbits were coming out to enjoy
the evening air. "Cousin Peter!" shouted
Benjamin Bunny. "He's bagged my
family – Tommy Brock – in a sack,
have you seen him?"

Peter had seen Tommy Brock,
carrying a sack with "something 'live in it".

"Tommy
Brock has
gone to Mr
Tod's other
house at the
top of Bull
Banks."

And Peter accompanied
the afflicted parent,
who was all of a twitter.
"Hurry, Peter; he will
be cooking them;
come quicker!" said
Benjamin Bunny.

186

Half way up the hill, Cotton-tail was sitting in her doorway. She had seen Tommy Brock passing. Benjamin and Peter climbed up and up.

"Squirrel Nutkin, have you seen Tommy Brock?" asked Peter. But he hadn't.

In the wood at Bull Banks, beneath a crag – Mr Tod had made one of his homes.

The rabbits crept up carefully. The setting sun made the window panels glow like red flame; but the kitchen fire was not alight. Benjamin sighed with relief. No person was to be seen, and no young rabbits. But the preparations for one person's supper on the table made

him shudder. They went round to the other side of the house, and crept up to the bedroom window. Tommy Brock was asleep in Mr Tod's bed.

They went back to the front of the house, and tried in vain to move the bolt of the kitchen window. In half an hour, the moon rose over the wood. In at the kitchen window, the light showed a little door belonging to a brick oven. Peter and Benjamin noticed that whenever they shook the window, the little door opposite shook in answer. The babies were alive, shut up in the oven!

There was really
not very much
comfort in the
discovery. The
little rabbits were
quite incapable
of letting
themselves out;
they were not old
enough to crawl.

Peter and Benjamin decided to dig a tunnel into the
kitchen. They dug and dug for hours and hours and by
the end of the night they were under the kitchen floor.
It was morning - sunrise.

From the fields down below there came the sharp yelping bark of a fox! Then those two rabbits did the most foolish thing that they could have done. They rushed into their short new tunnel, and hid themselves at the top end of it, under Mr Tod's kitchen floor.

Mr Tod was coming up Bull Banks. He was in the very worst of tempers. "I can smell Badger," he fumed, and slapped his stick upon the earth.

The sight of the table all set out for supper made Mr Tod furious. But what absorbed his attention was a noise - a deep slow snoring noise, coming from his own bed. He peeped around the bedroom door.

Mr Tod came out of the house in a hurry; he scratched up the earth with fury. His whiskers bristled and his coat-collar stood on end with rage. "Badger . . . Badger . . . in my house, in my bed, I'll fix that Badger." He fetched a clothes line and went back into the bedroom.

He watched Tommy
Brock and listened
to the loud snores.
Then he turned
his back towards the
bed and undid the
window. It creaked;
he turned round with
a jump. Tommy
Brock, who had
opened one eye –
shut it hastily.

Mr Tod pushed the
greater part of the
clothes line out of
the window.

He went out the
front door, took up
the coil of line
from the window
sill and tied the
rope to a tree.
A sly grin crept
across his face.

Mr Tod fetched a heavy
pailful of water and
staggered with it into his
bedroom. Tommy Brock
was lying on his back with
his mouth open, grinning
from ear to ear. One eye
was still not perfectly shut.

Then Mr Tod took up
the end of the rope with a
hook attached. He gingerly
mounted a chair by the
head of the bedstead. His
legs were dangerously near
to Tommy Brock's teeth.
He reached up and put
the end of the rope over
the head of the bed.

Mr Tod was quite unable
to lift the heavy weight of
the full pail of water to the
level of the hook and rope,
so he emptied the water
into a wash-basin and jug.

He slung up the empty pail wobbling over the head of Tommy Brock. Surely there never was such a sleeper!

As he could not lift the whole pailful of water at once, he fetched a milk jug, and ladled quarts of water into the pail. The pail got fuller and fuller . . .

At last Mr Tod's preparations were complete, and he softly left the room. He ran round behind the house, to the tree. He was obliged to gnaw the rope with his teeth – he chewed and gnawed for more than twenty minutes.

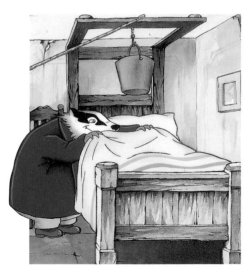

The moment he had gone, Tommy Brock got up in a hurry. He rolled Mr Tod's dressing-gown in to a bundle, put it into the bed under the covers, and left the room, grinning immensely.

Finally, the rope snapped. Inside the house there was a great crash and splash. But no screams. Mr Tod listened attentively. Then he peeped in at the window. In the middle of the bed under the blanket, was a wet flattened *something* – and it *was not snoring any longer.*

"This has turned out even better than I expected," said Mr Tod.

Mr Tod opened
the door . . .
Tommy Brock
was sitting at
Mr Tod's kitchen
table. He was
quite dry, and
he was grinning.
He threw a cup
of scalding tea
all over Mr Tod.
Then there
was a terrific
battle all over
the kitchen.

Benjamin and Peter crept out of their tunnel, and hung about amongst the rocks, listening anxiously.

Tommy Brock and Mr Tod rolled over the bank and down the hill, bumping over the rocks. There would never be any love lost between Tommy Brock and Mr Tod.

As soon as the coast was clear, Peter Rabbit and Benjamin Bunny came out of the bushes.

In Mr Tod's kitchen, amongst the wreckage, Benjamin Bunny picked his way to the oven nervously. He opened the oven door, felt inside, and found something warm and wriggling. He lifted it out carefully, and rejoined Peter Rabbit outside.

At home in the rabbit hole, things had not been comfortable. After quarrelling at supper, Flopsy and old Mr Bouncer had passed a sleepless night, and quarrelled again at breakfast.

Benjamin and Peter reached home safely and burst into the hole.

Great was old Mr Bouncer's relief and Flopsy's joy when Peter and Benjamin arrived in triumph with the young family.

"Oh, thank goodness you're all safe," said Flopsy.

Old Mr Bouncer was forgiven. The rabbit-babies were
fed and put to bed. They soon recovered. Then Peter
and Benjamin told their story - but they had not
waited long enough to be able to tell the end of the
battle between Tommy Brock and Mr Tod.

THE TALE OF
TWO BAD MICE
AND
JOHNNY TOWN-MOUSE

Once upon a time there was a very beautiful doll's-house.

It belonged to two dolls called Lucinda and Jane. Jane was the cook; but she never did any cooking, because the dinner had been bought

ready-made, in a box full of shavings.

One morning Lucinda and Jane went out for a drive in the doll's perambulator. There was no one in the nursery.

Presently, Tom Thumb and his wife, Hunca Munca, poked their heads out of the mouse-hole in the skirting board.

Tom Thumb and Hunca Munca went cautiously across the hearthrug. Hunca Munca pushed the front door - it was not locked. "Let's have a look inside," she said.

Tom Thumb and Hunca Munca went upstairs and peeped into the dining-room. Such a lovely dinner was laid out upon the table!

Tom Thumb set to work at once to carve the ham, but the knife crumpled up and hurt him. "It's not cooked enough. It's hard. You have a try Hunca Munca."

Hunca Munca stood up in her chair, and chopped at the ham. It broke off the plate with a jerk, and rolled under the table. "Let it alone," said Tom Thumb; "give me some fish, Hunca Munca!"

Hunca Munca tried every tin spoon in turn; the fish was glued to the dish.

Then Tom Thumb lost his temper. He hit the ham with the tongs and with the shovel. The ham flew all into pieces. Underneath the shiny paint it was made of nothing but plaster!

Then there was no end to their rage and disappointment. They broke up the pudding, the lobsters, the pears and the oranges. As the fish would not come off the plate, they put it into the red-hot crinkly paper fire in the kitchen; but it would not burn either.

Tom Thumb went up the chimney – there was no soot. Hunca Munca found some tiny cans upon the dresser, labelled Rice, Coffee, Sago, but there was nothing inside except red and blue beads.

Up in the bedroom, after pulling half the feathers out of Lucinda's bolster, Hunca Munca remembered that she herself needed a feather bed.

They carried the bolster downstairs and across the hearthrug. It was difficult to squeeze the bolster into the mouse-hole, but they managed it somehow.

"Now let's go back and see what else will be useful." said Hunca Munca.

They went back and fetched a chair, a book-case, a
bird-cage, and several odds and ends. The book-case and
the bird-cage would not go into the mouse-hole. Hunca
Munca left them behind the coal-box, and went to fetch
a cradle. "This will be fine for my babies," she said.

Hunca Munca was just returning with another chair, when suddenly there was a noise of talking outside upon the landing. The mice rushed back to their hole, and the dolls came into the nursery.

What a sight met their eyes!

The book-case and the bird-cage were rescued from under the coal-box, but Hunca Munca has got the cradle, and some of Lucinda's clothes.

She also has some useful pots and pans, and several other things.

The little girl said, "I will get a policeman doll!"
But her nurse said, "I will set a mouse-trap!"

Hunca Munca and Tom Thumb were not the only mice causing trouble that day.

When the cook opened the vegetable hamper, out sprang a terrified Timmy Willie.

"A mouse! A mouse! Call the cat!" screamed the cook.

But Timmy Willie did not wait for the cat. He rushed along the skirting board till he came to a little hole, and in he popped.

He dropped half a foot, and crashed into the middle of a mouse dinner-party, breaking three glasses.

"Who in the world is this?" inquired Johnny Town-mouse. But after the first exclamation of surprise, he instantly recovered his manners.

He introduced Timmy to nine other mice, all with long tails and white neck-ties. The dinner was truly elegant. Timmy was very anxious to behave with good manners, but the continual noise upstairs made him so nervous that he dropped a plate.

"Never mind," said Johnny.

"I'm from the country," said Timmy Willie. He explained how he had climbed into a hamper by the garden gate. After eating

some peas, he had fallen fast asleep. Then there was a jolting and a clattering of horses' feet. Timmy Willie awoke with a

fright. At last the cart stopped at a house and the hamper was carried in and set down. The cook lifted the hamper lid and screamed at the sight of poor Timmy Willie.

"Then I fell in here," finished Timmy.

Timmy Willie felt quite tired. "Would you like to go to bed?" said Johnny. "I will show you a most comfortable sofa pillow."

"It is the best bed and I keep it exclusively for visitors," said Johnny Town-mouse. But the sofa smelt of cat. Timmy Willie preferred to spend a miserable night under the fender.

"Oh dear, oh dear!" he sighed. "I wish I was home."

The next day things were no better for Timmy Willie. He could not eat the food, and the noise prevented him from sleeping.

"I do so miss my peaceful sunny bank and my friend, Cock Robin," said Timmy Willie.

"It may be that your teeth and digestion are unaccustomed to our food," said Johnny Town-mouse. "Perhaps it might be wiser for you to return in the hamper, to your own home in the country."

"Oh? Oh!" cried Timmy.

"Why of course. Did you not know that the hamper goes back empty on Saturdays?" said Johnny, rather huffily.

After much jolting, Timmy Willie was set down safely in his own garden.

"How good to be back!" said Timmy, in delight.

Sometimes he went to look at the hamper lying by the gate, but he knew better than to get in again. And nobody got out, though Johnny Town-mouse had half promised a visit.

Timmy Willie slept through the winter . . .

... and when Spring arrived, up the sandy path all spick and span with a brown leather bag came Johnny Town-mouse!

Timmy Willie received him with open arms. "You have come at the best of times. We will have herb pudding and sit in the sun."

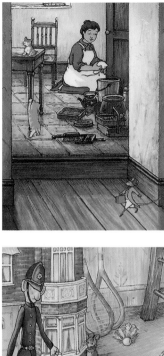

"How are Tom Thumb and all our friends?" asked Timmy.

Johnny explained the cook was doing spring cleaning, with particular instructions to clear out the mice. There were four kittens and the cat had killed the canary.

"Tom Thumb has told the mice all about the trap, and Hunca Munca has become friends with the policeman-doll, although he never says anything, and always looks quite stern," said Johnny.

The two friends were walking down the path, when Cock Robin flew down. "Hide!" shouted Johnny, in fright. "It's only my friend Cock Robin," said Timmy Willie. "Whatever is that fearful racket?" said Johnny Town-mouse.

"That's only the lawn-mower," said Timmy. "Now we can fetch some fresh grass clippings to make up your bed."

Johnny waited while Timmy went to fetch the milk and the fresh grass. When he returned, it began to rain. "Oh! My tail is getting all wet!" complained Johnny.

"It's only a spring shower. Here, take this leaf and hold it over your head like this," said Timmy.

"I am sure you will never want to live in town again," said Timmy Willie. But he did! He went back in the very next hamper of vegetables. He said it was too quiet.

Johnny got back safely to his town-house
and his old friends.

And the two bad mice were not so naughty after all. Tom Thumb found a sixpence; and upon Christmas Eve, he and Hunca Munca stuffed it into one of the stockings of Lucinda and Jane. And very early every morning, Hunca Munca comes with her dustpan and broom to sweep the dollies' house!

As for Timmy Willie, he stayed in the country and
he never went to town again. One place suits
one person, another place suits another person.
For my part I prefer to live in the country,
like Timmy Willie.

THE TALE OF
PIGLING BLAND

Old Aunt Pettitoes had a family of eight: four little girl pigs – Cross-patch, Suck-suck, Yock-yock and Spot; and four little boy pigs, – Alexander, Pigling Bland, Chin-chin and Stumpy.

The eight little pigs had very good appetites.

"I do believe I can't be coping much longer with my unruly brood," Aunt Pettitoes sighed. "They are indeed becoming a burden and a worry. Good little Spot shall stay at home to do the housework, but the others must go.

"Pigling Bland, you must go to market. You too, Alexander."

Aunt Pettitoes handed the two little pigs their licences permitting them to travel to market.

"Beware of hen roosts, bacon and eggs, and mind your Sunday clothes," she warned. "Take these eight conversation peppermints, and do heed the moral sentiments on them and you'll come to no harm."

Pigling Bland and Alexander set off for market.

They trotted along steadily for a mile, when Alexander began to feel hungry.

Alexander gobbled up his dinner and then asked for one of Pigling's peppermints. Pigling Bland said he wished to save them and held them out of reach.

There was a brief scuffle, and Pigling
Bland picked up the licences.

The two little pigs trotted along together, singing:

"Tom, Tom, the piper's son, stole a pig and away he ran."

"Oh!" Pigling Bland gasped suddenly and came to an abrupt halt.

"Where are your licences?"
the policeman demanded.

Pigling Bland pulled out his
paper; Alexander, after fumbling,
handed over something scrumply.

"This ain't a licence!"
said the policeman.
"I'll have to escort you
back to the farm."
And he led
Alexander away.

Pigling Bland continued on his
way dejectedly. He pulled his coat tightly round his
neck, and put his hands in his pockets to warm them.
"What's this?" he wondered. "Alexander's licence!"
He started to run back. "Oh, Mr Policeman!
I've found the licence!"

But Pigling Bland took several wrong turns and very soon he was quite lost. The wind whistled and the trees creaked and Pigling began to feel frightened.

"I can't find my way home!" Pigling cried. "Wherever can I be? I can go no further tonight I fear. I must find some-where to rest for the night and shelter from this wind."

Then past the edge of a wood Pigling saw a small wooden hen house and crept inside.

He squeezed between two hens. "Bacon and eggs! Bacon and eggs!" clucked the hens.

Pigling Bland curled up and fell fast asleep.

Suddenly, the door creaked open. The bright light from a lantern shone into Pigling's face. It was the farmer, Mr Piperson.

"I need six of you fowl to take to market in the morning," he whispered to himself, grabbing a hen roughly.

"Here's another!" said Mr Piperson, seizing Pigling by the scruff of the neck and dropping him into the hamper.

Then he dropped five more dirty, kicking, cackling hens upon the top of Pigling Bland.

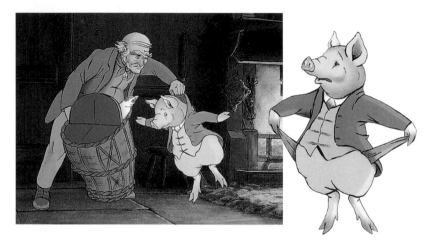

Back at the farm kitchen, Mr Piperson lifted Pigling out of the hamper.

"I am but a poor little pig," said Pigling, showing his empty pockets.

"You may stay for supper," said the farmer.

Pigling Bland sat on a stool by the fire whilst Mr Piperson pulled off his boots and threw them into a corner.

As they hit the wainscot there was a smothered noise.

"Shut up!" growled Mr Piperson to the noise. It seemed to Pigling that something at the further end of the kitchen was taking a suppressed interest in the cooking.

Mr Piperson poured out three platefuls of porridge: one for himself, one for Pigling and a third. Pigling ate his supper discreetly.

After supper Mr Piperson consulted an almanac and looked at Pigling. Then he prodded Pigling's ribs.

"It's too late in the season for curing bacon," he muttered to himself.

Then he turned to Pigling. "Oh, well, you may sleep on the rug," he said.

The next morning there was a whistle from outside. It was Mr Piperson's neighbour, come to take him to market. "Now shut the door behind me," ordered Mr Piperson.

"And don't meddle with anything, or I'll skin ye!" said Mr Piperson menacingly.

Back inside, Pigling finished off his breakfast and began to sing to himself. Suddenly a little smothered voice chimed in.

Pigling listened carefully and went round the kitchen searching for the voice. Then he came to a locked cupboard. He pushed a peppermint under the door. It was sucked in immediately. He pushed in his last six peppermints, and they were all sucked up.

"So, how's Mr Piggy-wiggy, then?" asked Mr Piperson when he returned from market.

"I must admit to being a little hungry," Pigling answered.

Mr Piperson prodded him in the ribs again.

"You feel nice and fat to me," he said laughing. "Well, then, I had better fix some supper for us."

After supper, Mr Piperson went to bed and Pigling Bland sat by the fire, eating his porridge.

All at once
a little
voice
spoke:

"My name is Pig-wig.
Make me some more
porridge please!"
Pigling was rather
startled. "How did
you come here?" he
asked, handing Pig-wig
his porridge.

"Stolen," replied
Pig-wig with her
mouth full.

Pigling wondered why
Pig-wig didn't run away.
But Pig-wig didn't seem
to know her way home.

"I'm going to market,"
Pigling said. "I have two pig
papers. Come with me!"

"How wonderfully kind!"
exclaimed Pig-wig.

She started to sing
and very soon she was
fast asleep.

Early the next morning Pigling tied up his little bundle and woke Pig-wig.

"Come along, Pig-wig. It's time for us to be on our way," he whispered.

"But it's so dark," complained Pig-wig.

"Come away," urged Pigling. "We will be able to see when we get used to it!"

Pigling Bland and Pig-wig slipped away hand in hand across an untidy field to the road.

They continued along the lane, hiding behind a wall as they passed a ploughman in a nearby field.

But suddenly Pigling stopped. Slowly jogging up the road came the grocer's cart.

"We may have to run," said Pigling. "Don't say a word. Leave it to me."

"Where are you two going?" demanded the grocer. "Are you going to market? Show me your licences."

The grocer looked at their licences.

"I'm not sure," he said, looking suspiciously at Pig-wig. He consulted the "Lost, Stolen or Strayed" section of his newspaper. "Just you wait here," he warned, and went to consult the ploughman.

Pigling and Pig-wig waited for a moment - and then off they raced! They ran down the hill till they came to the river. They reached the bridge and crossed it hand in hand.

"Freedom! Safety!" cried Pigling happily.

262

Then over the hills and far away, Pig-wig danced with Pigling Bland. As they danced they sang a tune:

"Tom, Tom, the piper's son,
Stole a pig and away he ran
And all the tune that he
could play
Was *over the hills and far away!*"

About The World of Peter Rabbit & Friends

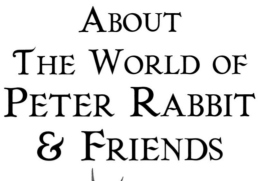

The illustrations in this book are taken from
The World of Peter Rabbit & Friends, a series
of animated films made for television and
video. On the following pages you can find
out how Beatrix Potter's stories were
turned into films.

THE MAKING OF AN ANIMATED FILM

An animated film is made up of thousands of separate still pictures. Each picture is called a 'frame' and each frame shows a gradually different stage in a movement. Every frame is photographed in sequence and then speeded up to flash past your eyes. This is how Peter Rabbit made his way from book to screen.

1. SCRIPT

Although the stories already exist, a writer has to adapt the tales to make them more suitable as films, bringing the characters alive. The script contains speech ('dialogue') and some camera instructions.

2. CHARACTER MODELS

Using Beatrix Potter's illustrations of animals, rough sketches are produced from which 'character models' are developed.

This rough character model sheet shows Peter Rabbit from all angles

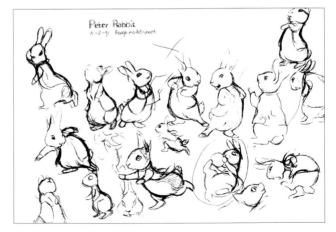

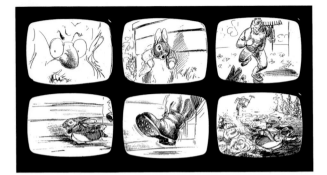

This storyboard gives an outline of one scene within the film

3. STORYBOARD
A storyboard looks like a comic strip and tells the story frame by frame. It enables the director and animators to visualise the story.

The storyboard frames are often accompanied by a line of dialogue or notes about the action.

4. SOUND TRACK
A sound track is made up of the voice track, the music track and the sound effects track – all recorded separately. The voice track is recorded first. Each noise will span a number of frames – this is recorded on a special document called a dopesheet. This will be used later by the animators to ensure that the mouth movements of the characters match up with what they are saying.

Meanwhile the composer writes music for the film, which is recorded on a music track. And finally, the sound effects are added.

5. THE ANIMATOR
The animator works on the drawings necessary to 'describe' the action.

Using the script, character models, sound track and dopesheet, the animator begins by making 'key drawings' (the first and last drawings of a movement).

6. THE INBETWEENER

Additional drawings needed to smooth out the action between the key drawings are produced by an 'inbetweener'. These lines drawings are now filmed to test that the action works properly.

7. TRACE AND PAINT

Trace and paint artists trace the drawings from paper on to clear plastic sheets, called cels. The colour is then painted on the back of the cels to make sure it is flat and even. The finishing touch is a special 'rendered layer' - this is a process which softens the outlines and adds textures with fine pencil and crayon giving the characters a three-dimensional effect.

Here, a cel on a background makes up the finished frame

8. BACKGROUNDS

The background is the painting on which a cel will be placed to create the complete scene. The artist refers closely to Beatrix Potter's drawings, the script and the storyboard.

9. FILMING

The 'checker' makes sure that all the cels needed are in the correct order, and that all the backgrounds match with the proper scenes. The cameraman then photographs the cels in sequence.

The cameraman also works out all the camera movements (close-ups, zooms, or fades) guided by the animator's instructions on the dopesheet.

The film is processed and an extra copy is made. This is called a work print and is passed to the editors, whilst the first 'master' copy of the film is kept safely.

10. THE EDITORS

The editors put all the different scenes of the film into the right order. They snip off little pieces of scenes that are too long, or add footage if a scene is too short.

They also match the sound track to the action. The master copy of the film is then cut carefully to match the edited version and printed together with the sound track to produce the finished film!

There are 24 illustrations per second of film